FACE
TO FACE
WITH
SCIENCE™

SALLY RIDE
TAM O'SHAUGHNESSY

VOYAGER

An Adventure

to the Edge

of the

Solar System

CROWN PUBLISHERS, INC. • New York

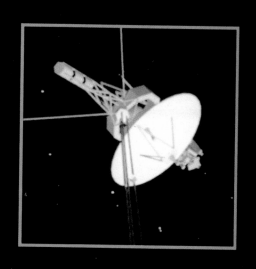

This is the story
of two spacecraft:
Voyager 1 and *Voyager* 2.
They were launched from Earth
to explore four distant planets:
Jupiter, Saturn, Uranus,
and Neptune.

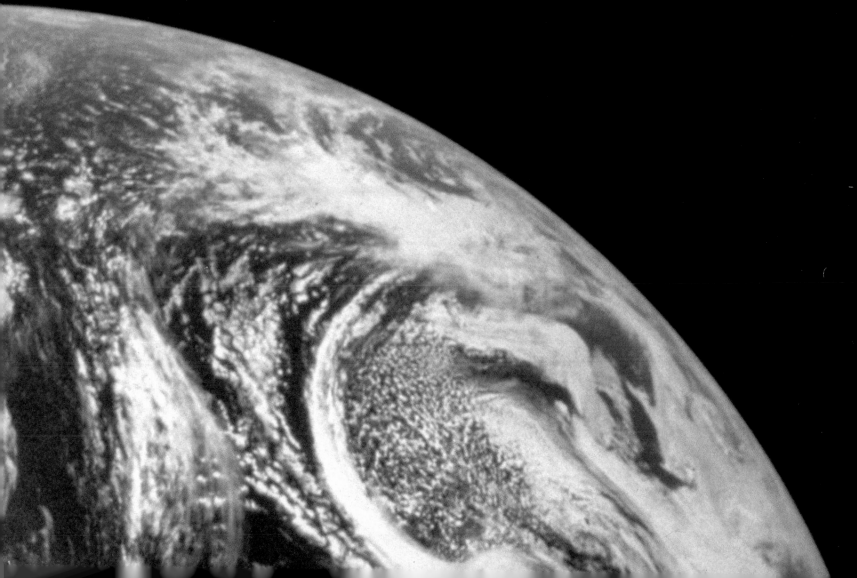

Earth is the third of nine planets that circle the star we call the Sun. Jupiter, Saturn, Uranus, and Neptune are the fifth, sixth, seventh, and eighth. They are very, very far away. Jupiter, even when it is closest to Earth, is 400 million miles away. Neptune is 3 billion miles away.

All four of these planets are very different from Earth.

The first two, Jupiter and Saturn, are like each other in many ways. Both of them are huge. Jupiter is the biggest planet in the solar system—more than one thousand Earths would fit inside it. Both are made up mostly of hydrogen and helium gas, the two lightest gases in the universe. Toward the center of each planet the gas gets thicker and thicker, until it is so thick that it becomes liquid. Jupiter and Saturn have no solid ground to stand on. Because they are so big, and are made up mostly of gas, they are called "gas giants."

The four giant planets, Jupiter, Saturn, Uranus, and Neptune, shown to scale. Earth (*below*) is also shown to scale.

Uranus and Neptune are also giant planets. Although they are not as big as Jupiter and Saturn, both are much, much bigger than Earth. Their atmospheres are also made up mostly of hydrogen and helium gas. Because they are so far away from the Sun, they are cold, dark planets.

Scientists had studied the four giant planets through telescopes and learned a lot about them, but even the most powerful telescopes could not answer all their questions. A spacecraft designed to explore the giant planets would give them a closer view. But it would have been impossible to send astronauts so far. Astronauts have never traveled beyond our own moon. A trip to the giant planets would be thousands of times farther and would take several years. Only a robot spacecraft could make the long journey.

The mission was so important that two spacecraft were built, *Voyager* 1 and *Voyager* 2. If one broke down on the long trip, there would still be one left.

The *Voyager*s were not very big—each one was about the size of a small car—but they were the most advanced spacecraft ever designed. The scientific instruments they carried included special cameras with telescopic lenses. These cameras would take close-up pictures of the giant planets and the surfaces of their moons. Other instruments would measure ultraviolet and infrared light. This light, invisible to normal cameras, would tell scientists more about the temperatures of the planets and what they are made of.

During their long trip through space, the *Voyager*s would be controlled from Earth. Scientists would radio commands to the spacecraft telling them what path to follow, what to photograph, and when to send back information. The *Voyager*s' antennas would always be pointed toward Earth, ready to receive instructions.

The pictures and information collected by the spacecraft would be radioed back to Earth. But the *Voyager*s' radio transmitters were not very powerful, and by the time their signals reached Earth, they would be very, very weak. Many large antennas all over the world would be needed to pick them up. It would be like listening for a whisper from thousands of miles away.

MISSION CONTROL

► Radio signals from the *Voyager*s were picked up by large antennas in California, Australia, and Spain. The signals were then relayed by satellite to Mission Control in Pasadena, California.

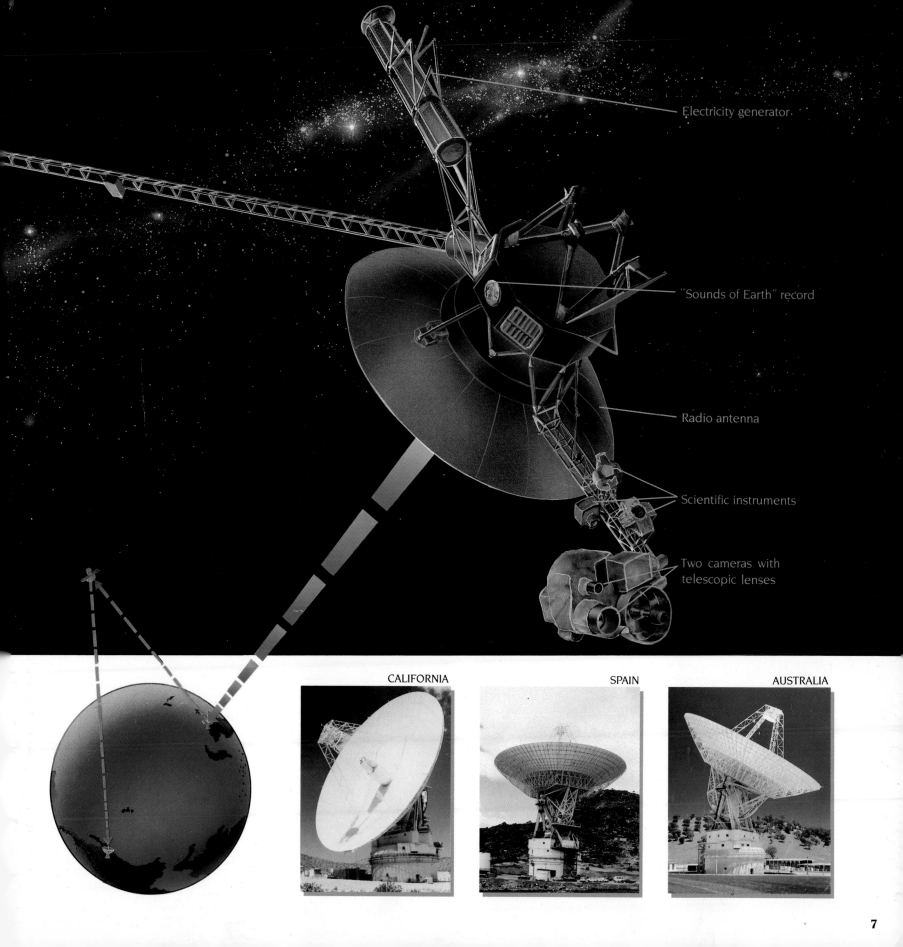

Electricity generator.

"Sounds of Earth" record

Radio antenna

Scientific instruments

Two cameras with telescopic lenses

CALIFORNIA

SPAIN

AUSTRALIA

Exploring all four giant planets is possible only when the planets are lined up correctly in their orbits. Then each planet's gravity can be used—like a slingshot—to speed up the spacecraft and bend its path toward the next planet. The *Voyagers* would fly to Jupiter, then use Jupiter's gravity to accelerate them toward Saturn. If both *Voyagers* were still working when they got to Saturn, one spacecraft would be sent to study Saturn's largest moon, Titan, and the other would continue on to explore Uranus and Neptune.

The planets do not line up this way often—only once every 176 years! The *Voyager* mission was a rare opportunity.

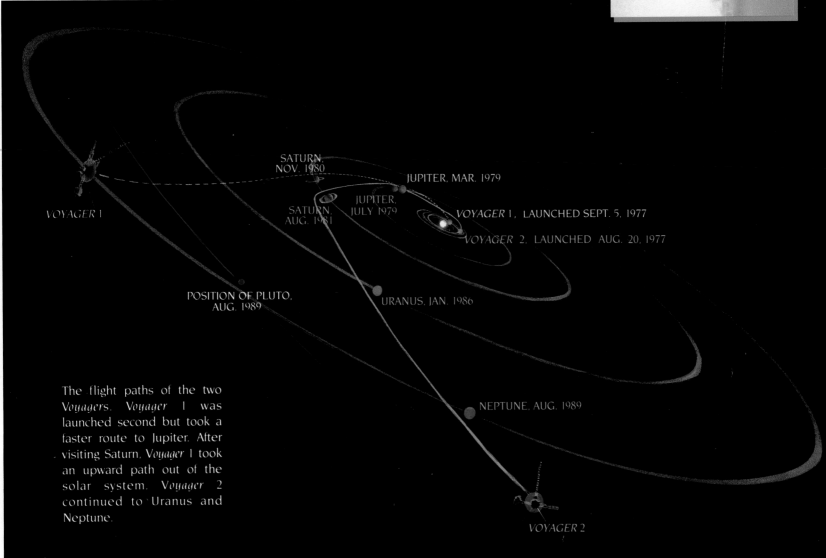

SATURN,
NOV. 1980

JUPITER, MAR. 1979

JUPITER,
JULY 1979

VOYAGER 1

SATURN,
AUG. 1981

VOYAGER 1, LAUNCHED SEPT. 5, 1977

VOYAGER 2, LAUNCHED AUG. 20, 1977

POSITION OF PLUTO,
AUG. 1989

URANUS, JAN. 1986

NEPTUNE, AUG. 1989

The flight paths of the two *Voyagers*. *Voyager* 1 was launched second but took a faster route to Jupiter. After visiting Saturn, *Voyager* 1 took an upward path out of the solar system. *Voyager* 2 continued to Uranus and Neptune.

VOYAGER 2

In the summer of 1977, the *Voyagers* were launched into space by two powerful rockets. Leaving Earth, they were flying so fast that it took them only ten hours to pass the Moon. As it was racing away, *Voyager* 1 looked back to take this picture of the Earth and Moon it was leaving behind.

On their way to Jupiter, the two *Voyagers* would have to pass through the asteroid belt. Asteroids are huge, fast-moving rocks that orbit around the Sun. There are thousands of them between the planets Mars and Jupiter, and a collision with one could destroy the spacecraft. Both *Voyagers* made it safely past them. *Voyager* 1 led the way to Jupiter, the first gas giant.

The Voyagers sped closer and closer to Jupiter. As the spacecraft approached the planet, hundreds of scientists crowded into Mission Control to see the close-up pictures of this faraway world.

The radio signals that carry Voyagers' pictures travel at the speed of light. So although it had taken the Voyagers one and a half years to travel to Jupiter, their pictures traveled back to Earth in about 45 minutes. As soon as the pictures were received by the huge antennas on Earth, they were relayed to Mission Control, then displayed on TV screens. The scientists were stunned by what they saw.

The giant planet has bright colors and complex patterns that scientists had never seen through their telescopes. It is covered with wide bands of yellow, orange, red, and white clouds. Violent storms move through the clouds.

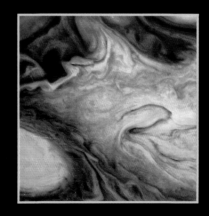

The Great Red Spot is a huge storm in Jupiter's atmosphere that never disappears. Scientists had looked at it through telescopes for over three hundred years, but they had never been able to study its motion. Hundreds of the *Voyagers'* pictures were put together into a movie so that the motions of the Great Red Spot and the other storms could be seen. The movie showed the Great Red Spot swirling violently around its center, with hurricane-force winds around its edges.

Each of the smaller white circles is also a violent, swirling storm. Scientists do not understand why some storms are bright red and others are white. Although the white storms look small next to the Great Red Spot, some of them are as big as the Earth.

Jupiter has 16 moons that circle around it like a miniature solar system. Three of these moons were discovered by the *Voyagers*. Some of the other moons were seen close up for the first time.

► Two pictures of Jupiter's Great Red Spot. The distance from top to bottom in the lower picture is about 15,000 miles.

Jupiter's moon Callisto has been hit by rocks and meteorites for over 4 billion years. Each of these collisions left a crater in Callisto's icy surface. Some of the craters look very bright. These are the newer ones. Each collision sprays fresh ice over the surface, and the freshest ice is the brightest.

Long ago, a very big object—maybe an asteroid—crashed into Callisto. Callisto's icy surface wasn't strong enough to hold the shape of the huge crater left by the collision. Its surface sagged back to its original shape, and now all that's left is a bright patch of ice and a series of faint rings that formed at the time of the collision.

CALLISTO

▼ Callisto's surface, showing thousands of craters and the bright patch of ice and faint rings left by a collision with another object.

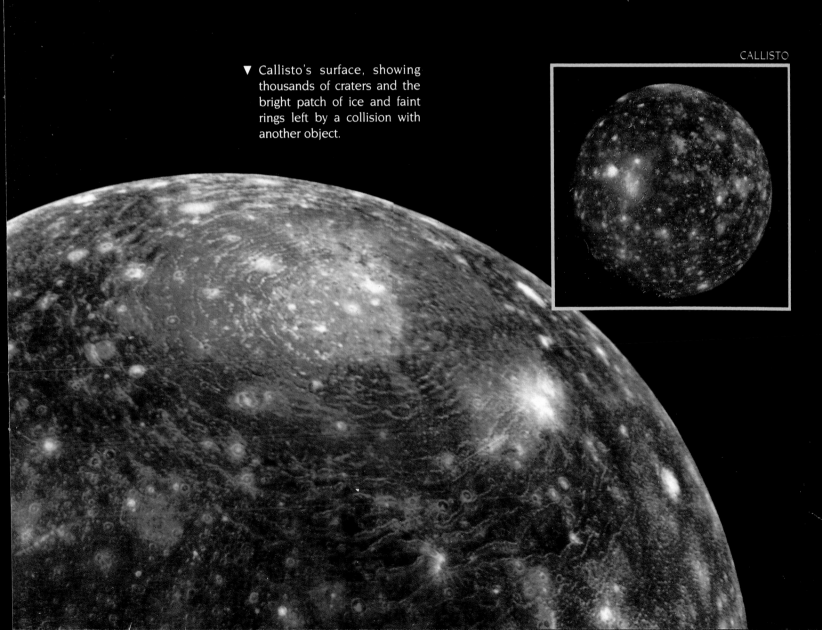

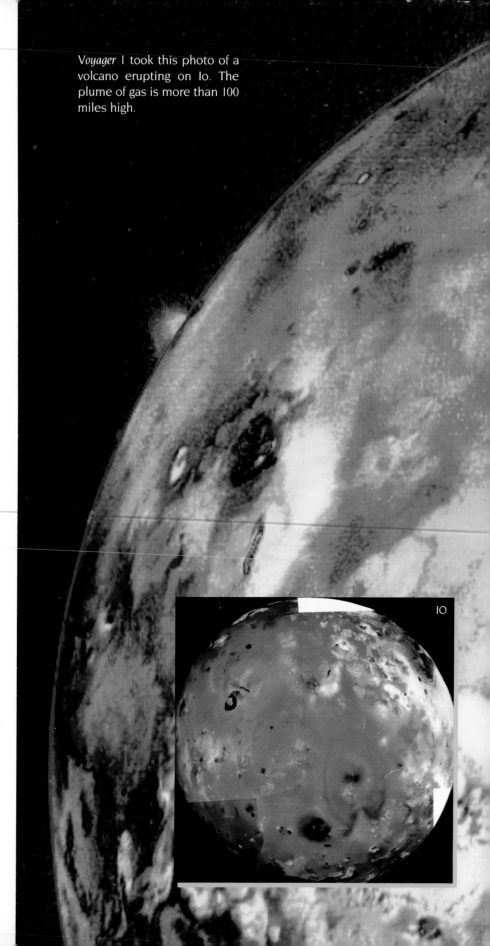

Scientists expected most of the moons in the solar system to look like Callisto—dark, frozen, and covered with craters. They were shocked when they saw the *Voyagers'* pictures of Io, another of Jupiter's moons. There were no craters, and its surface looked orange and splotchy. At first Io was a mystery. But then one of the *Voyagers'* pictures showed something completely unexpected: a volcano erupting! There are active volcanoes on Earth, but scientists did not expect to find them anywhere else in the solar system. Nine volcanoes were erupting on Io while the *Voyagers* flew past, some throwing hot gas hundreds of miles high. There are no craters on Io because lava from the volcanoes flows over its surface and fills in the craters. The cooled lava contains the chemical sulfur, which gives Io's surface its orange, yellow, red, and black colors.

Europa is Jupiter's brightest moon. Like Io, Europa did not look the way scientists expected a moon to look. It is bright because it is covered with a very smooth layer of ice that reflects the sunlight. Scientists believe that the lines on Europa's surface are cracks in the ice. Fresh ice from below the surface oozes up through the cracks and forms long, flat ridges.

Voyager I took this photo of a volcano erupting on Io. The plume of gas is more than 100 miles high.

Io

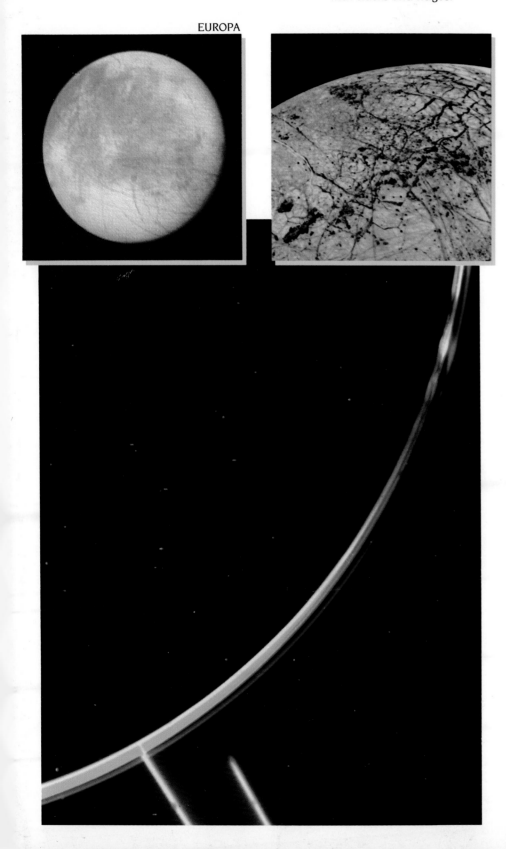

▼ Europa's icy surface, covered with cracks and ridges.

EUROPA

◄ Jupiter's ring (*at the bottom of the picture*), lit by sunlight coming from behind the planet.

Like Callisto, Europa has been hit by thousands of rocks and meteorites. But there are very few craters left on its surface. Europa's layer of ice must have once been soft, or even liquid, and erased the craters.

For hundreds of years, scientists thought that Saturn was the only planet with rings, but the Voyagers discovered a thin ring around Jupiter. The ring could not be seen from Earth. Even the Voyagers' sensitive cameras could barely make it out.

The ring is made up of very small dust particles that are circling the planet. Where does the dust come from? The Voyagers discovered two tiny moons at the edge of the ring. Scientists think that meteorites hit those moons and knock dust off their surfaces. The dust goes into orbit around the planet and becomes part of the ring.

The Voyagers relayed more than 30,000 pictures of Jupiter and its moons back to Earth. As scientists settled down to study the pictures and other scientific information, the spacecraft began their two-year trip to the next planet, Saturn.

SATURN

Saturn is the second largest planet in the solar system—only Jupiter is bigger. But although Saturn is big, it is very light. It is not like a big rock. A rock would sink in a bucket of water. If you could find a bucket big enough, Saturn would float in it.

When astronomers look at Saturn through telescopes on Earth, they see a yellow, hazy planet with three beautiful rings. But as the *Voyagers* got closer and closer, they showed Saturn as it had never been seen before. The planet turned out to have broad belts of brown, yellow, and orange clouds. Its striped atmosphere reminded scientists of Jupiter, but the colors weren't as bright, and the bands weren't as sharp.

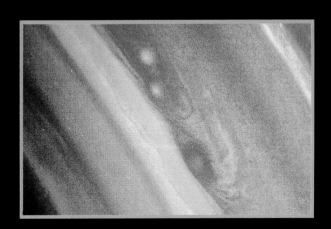

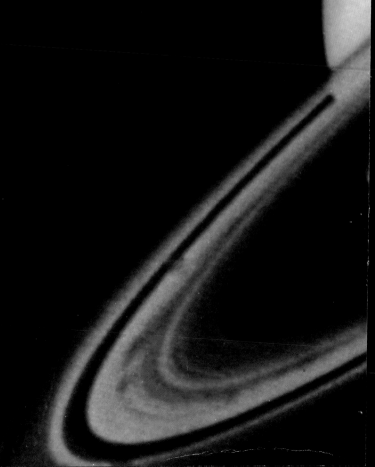

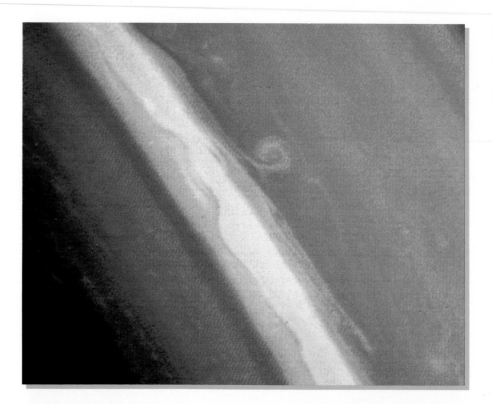

▶ Saturn's atmosphere, photographed by *Voyager* 2. The white band is moving at more than 300 miles per hour.

High winds howl through Saturn's atmosphere, blowing much faster than any winds on Earth. Jet streams near Saturn's equator can reach 1,000 miles per hour. The *Voyager*s also discovered wild, swirling storms, like those in Jupiter's atmosphere.

Saturn's famous rings are made up of countless pieces of rock and ice in high-speed orbits around the planet. If you could scoop up all the particles in the rings, you would have enough rock and ice to make a medium-sized moon. Scientists think that the rings may be what's left of a moon that was shattered by collisions.

As part of an experiment, the *Voyager*s sent radio signals through the rings back to Earth. The radio signals were changed a little bit as they went through the rings. By studying these changes, scientists learned that the pieces of rock and ice that make up the rings come in many different sizes. Some are as small as grains of sand. Some are as big as trucks.

▲ ▶ Saturn's rings. Colors have been added to the photographs by a computer to show different parts of the rings.

◄ This picture shows Saturn, its rings, and two of its 18 moons, Tethys and Dione.

From Earth, Saturn appears to have three broad rings. In the *Voyagers'* pictures it looked as if there were thousands and thousands of rings. *Voyagers'* other instruments showed that the rings are all part of a huge sheet of particles. There are no completely empty gaps. The thin sheet starts close to Saturn's cloud tops and extends out 40,000 miles. Three very faint rings orbit outside the main sheet.

The *Voyagers* discovered a very small moon, invisible from Earth, at the outer edge of the main sheet of rings. This moon, like the rings themselves, is probably a piece of a larger moon that was shattered when it was hit by a comet or an asteroid. There are other small moons like this one that help shape the rings and sweep the edges clean.

Saturn has at least 18 moons, more than any other planet. Four of them, including the one at the edge of the main sheet of rings, were discovered by the *Voyagers*.

The *Voyagers'* pictures of Saturn's moons show that the solar system can be a dangerous place. One of the moons, Mimas, barely survived a collision that left an enormous crater on its surface. The crater is 80 miles wide, and the mountain at its center is higher than Mount Everest. If the collision had been much harder, Mimas would have split apart.

Another moon, Hyperion, is probably a piece of what was once a larger moon that did break apart.

Most of Saturn's moons are icy balls that were formed at the same time as the planet. But Phoebe is different. It is probably an asteroid that came too close to the planet and was captured by the pull of Saturn's gravity. The picture is blurry because Phoebe is small and *Voyager* was far away.

Titan, Saturn's largest moon, fascinated scientists. Before the *Voyager* mission, it was the only moon in the solar system known to have an atmosphere. From Earth, scientists had detected methane gas around Titan, but they could not tell whether there were other gases in its atmosphere. To find out more, scientists sent *Voyager* 1 on a path that would take it very close to this unusual moon.

MIMAS
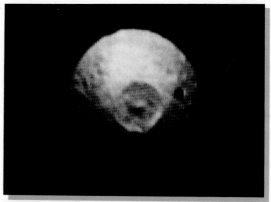

HYPERION
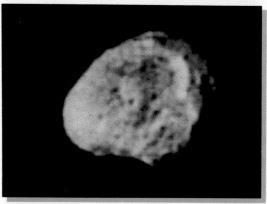

PHOEBE
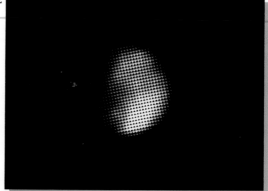

TITAN
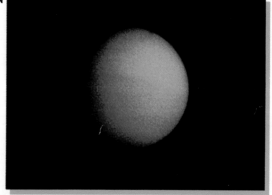

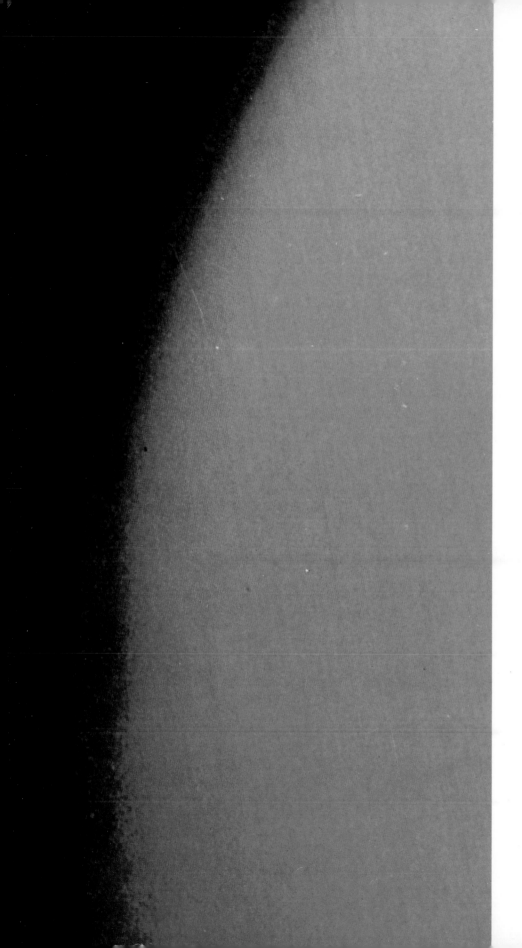

When the spacecraft arrived at Titan, it found a thick orange haze covering the moon. Titan's atmosphere is very thick—more than one and a half times thicker than the air on Earth. It is made up mostly of nitrogen gas, just like Earth's atmosphere. But unlike the air we breathe, Titan's atmosphere contains no oxygen.

What is below the orange haze? *Voyager* 1's cameras could not see to Titan's surface, but its other instruments sent back clues. The chemical ethane is as abundant on Titan as water is on Earth. Scientists think that Titan might have ethane rainstorms, and maybe even ethane rivers and lakes on its frozen surface.

Because *Voyager* 1's path took it so close to Titan, it would not be able to go on to Uranus and Neptune. Instead, the spacecraft headed up and out of the main plane of the solar system.

Voyager 2 was on a path that would enable it to visit the last two giant planets. Using Saturn's gravity like a giant slingshot, *Voyager* 2 said good-bye to its twin and headed for Uranus alone.

◄This photograph of Titan's hazy atmosphere was taken from a distance of 270,000 miles.

URANUS

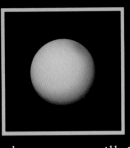

Uranus is so far
away that it took
Voyager 2 more than
four years to travel
there from Saturn. The
planet was still 150 million miles away
when *Voyager* took this picture.

Because Uranus is so far from the
Sun, it does not get much heat or
light. It is a cold, dark planet. Taking
pictures at Uranus is like taking
pictures at twilight on Earth. So as
Voyager approached Uranus, scientists
adjusted its cameras to take pictures in
this dim light.

Voyager got closer and closer to the
planet, but all the pictures relayed
back to Earth looked the same. Uranus
does not have streaming bands of
color or swirling storms like Jupiter and
Saturn. Its pale blue atmosphere is
almost featureless. *Voyager* did measure
strong winds, but they are not as
strong as the winds on the other two
planets.

Uranus' atmosphere is made up mostly of hydrogen and helium gas, like Jupiter and Saturn. But it also has small amounts of methane. It is the methane that gives Uranus its blue color.

Although this pale blue planet looks calm and peaceful, scientists think it had a violent past. Early in its history, Uranus probably collided with a huge object, maybe a comet the size of Earth. This collision was so violent that Uranus was knocked over. Now the planet lies on its side. As it orbits around the Sun, first its south pole then its north pole point toward the Sun.

The same year that the Voyagers were launched from Earth, scientists looking through telescopes discovered nine narrow rings around Uranus. When Voyager 2 got there, it found two more.

▶ Colors have been added to this picture of Uranus by a computer. Areas near the planet's south pole were warmer at the time of Voyager's approach because they were facing the sun. These areas are shown in yellow and orange.

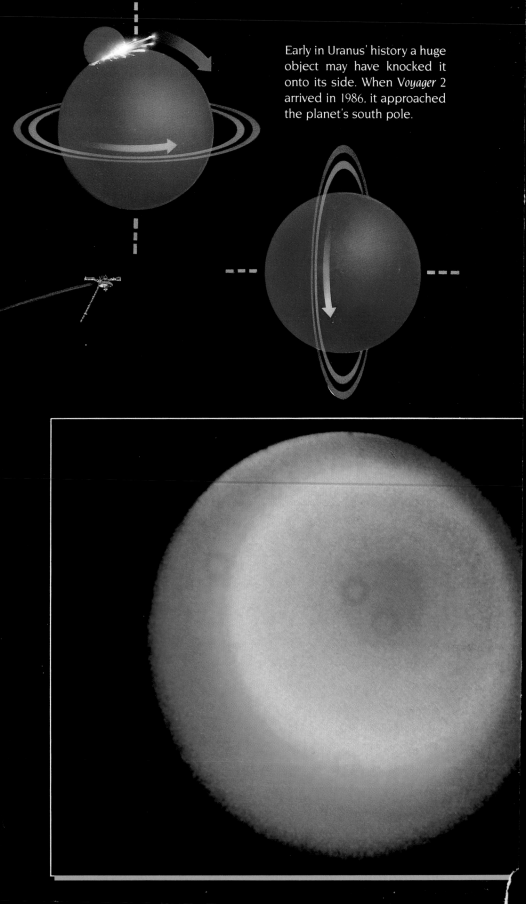

Early in Uranus' history a huge object may have knocked it onto its side. When Voyager 2 arrived in 1986, it approached the planet's south pole.

Uranus' rings are very different from both the faint ring around Jupiter and the broad sheet of rings around Saturn. The rings of Jupiter and Saturn have many tiny particles in them, but Uranus' rings seem to be made up mostly of big chunks of rock and ice the size of boulders. Scientists were puzzled. Shouldn't the boulders crash into each other and break into smaller pieces? Scientists are still studying the information *Voyager* sent back, looking for the small particles they think should be there.

The rings are also much darker than those of Jupiter and Saturn. The boulders in Uranus' rings are as black as charcoal.

The picture below, and a picture like it from Saturn, gave scientists a clue to the mystery of what holds a ring together. Because of *Voyager*'s photographs, scientists now think that particles can be held in the shape of a ring by two small moons, one on each side of the ring. Each moon's gravity pulls on the particles in a kind of tug-of-war, which keeps the particles in a ring between them.

The *Voyager*s showed that moons and rings are closely related. Not only can rings be held in place by small moons, but the rings themselves may be what's left of moons that were shattered by collisions with comets or asteroids.

◀ Uranus' rings. The two rings *Voyager* discovered are so faint that they don't show up in this picture.

▲ Two tiny moons (*circled*), close to one of Uranus' rings.

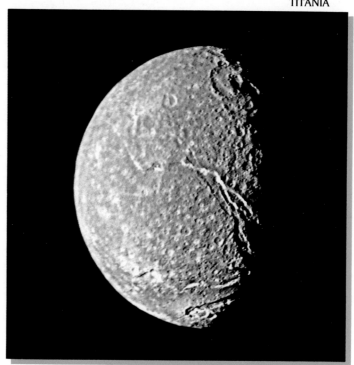

Before *Voyager* 2 visited Uranus, scientists had found five moons around the planet, but they did not know how big they were, or what they were made of. In just a few hours, *Voyager* discovered ten new moons. It found that Uranus' moons are made up mostly of ice and rock, and that even its largest moons, Titania and Oberon, are only half the size of Earth's moon.

Miranda is the closest moon to the planet. It looks like a jigsaw puzzle whose pieces have been scrambled. Part of its surface looks old and cratered, and part of it looks young and very rough. There are ice cliffs ten miles high and canyons ten miles deep. Scientists are puzzled by Miranda. Some think it is possible that Miranda was once torn apart by a collision. The pieces stayed in orbit around Uranus and were slowly drawn back together to form a moon again. This theory could explain the mixed-up appearance of the moon we see today.

OBERON

MIRANDA

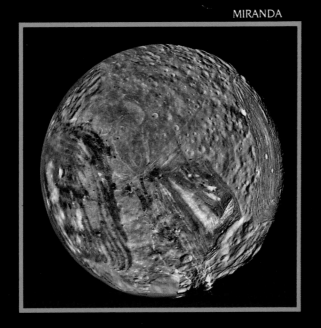

▼ Part of Miranda's surface.

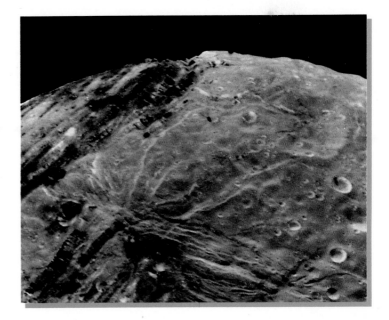

Voyager 2's encounter with Uranus was very short. Most pictures of the planet, its rings, and its moons were taken in only six hours. But those six hours gave scientists their first real look at this pale blue planet.

After traveling nearly 3 billion miles, Voyager still had 1½ billion miles to go before reaching Neptune, the last giant planet in our solar system.

◄ Voyager looked back to take this farewell picture of Uranus from a distance of 600,000 miles.

NEPTUNE

Voyager 2 had been traveling for 12 years. The aging spacecraft had survived its long trip through space and was finally nearing Neptune. There was great excitement in Mission Control. Scientists had waited a long time for a close look at this mysterious planet.

Voyager did not disappoint them. In the very first close-up pictures, scientists discovered a new moon orbiting close to Neptune. The moon is small, dark, and bumpy. It looks as if it has lived through many collisions. Voyager would discover five more small moons before it left Neptune.

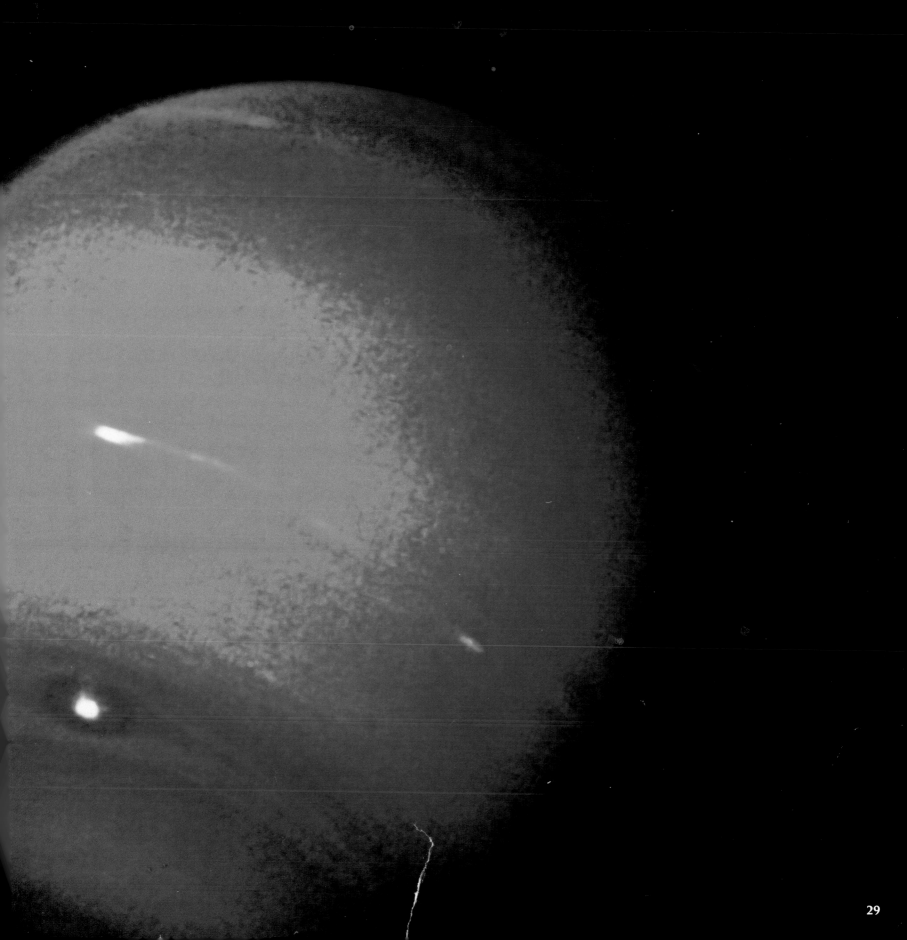

Voyager's next pictures brought another discovery: there are rings around this planet, too. Two are narrow, and two are broad. The particles that make up Neptune's rings are small, like those in Jupiter's rings. But they are also very black, like the big boulders circling Uranus.

Neptune's rings are unusual because some parts of them are thicker than others. The particles in the rings are not spread out evenly. Scientists do not understand why. There might be very small moons shaping the rings, but none have yet been found.

Scientists expected Neptune to be a lot like Uranus because the two planets are about the same size and are very, very far away from the Sun. But *Voyager*'s pictures surprised them. This cold, blue planet has violent weather. Its atmosphere has wild storms, like those on Jupiter and Saturn.

One huge storm was named the Great Dark Spot because it reminded scientists of Jupiter's Great Red Spot. Winds near its edges are the strongest measured on any planet—over 1,400 miles per hour!

▼ Two photographs were combined to make this picture of Neptune's rings.

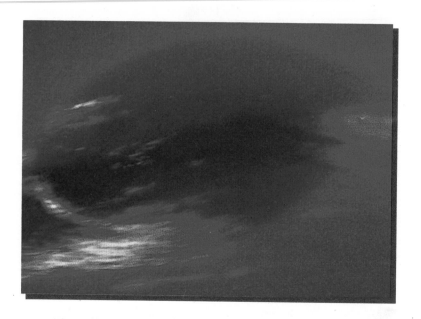

▲ A close-up picture of the Great Dark Spot.

► A more distant view of Neptune, showing the Great Dark Spot and a smaller storm to the south.

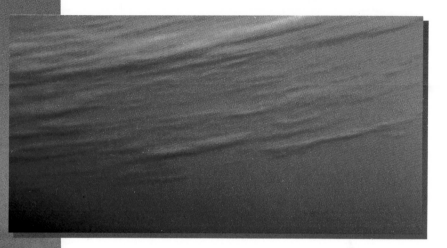

▼ White clouds high in Neptune's atmosphere cast dark shadows on the blue cloud layer below.

Voyager flew closer to Neptune than to any other planet, skimming only three thousand miles above the tops of its clouds. The white clouds in Neptune's atmosphere look like high, thin clouds on Earth. You can see their dark shadows on the cloud layer below. From the shadows, scientists figured out that the white clouds are floating many miles above the others.

Voyager's flight path also took it very close to Neptune's rings. As it passed the rings, it was hit again and again by tiny dust particles. Even though the particles were very small, they were moving so fast that *Voyager* could have been damaged. But the bombardment lasted only a few moments, and *Voyager* made it safely past. *Voyager* raced toward its last target, Neptune's largest moon, Triton.

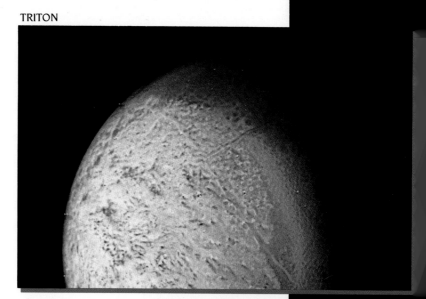

Very little was known about Triton, but observations from Earth led scientists to believe that it might have an atmosphere. *Voyager* found that it does. Triton's atmosphere is made up of the same gases—nitrogen and methane—as the atmosphere of Saturn's moon, Titan. But Triton's atmosphere is very, very thin. *Voyager's* cameras could easily see through it to the moon's surface.

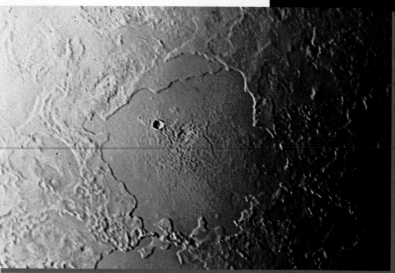

Most moons are formed with their planet, so they orbit in the same direction as the planet spins. Triton orbits Neptune in the "wrong" direction. This makes scientists think that Triton was formed somewhere else in the solar system but came too close to Neptune and was captured by the planet's gravity.

After Triton was captured, the forces pulling it toward Neptune may have heated Triton and melted it. It is possible that for a billion years Triton was a liquid moon. Today, Triton is the coldest place in the solar system—its temperature is 390 degrees (Fahrenheit) below zero. Its surface is frozen hard.

► *Center:* Part of Triton's surface. The distance across the photograph is about 300 miles. *Bottom:* Part of the ice cap at Triton's south pole. The dark smudges may be ice geysers.

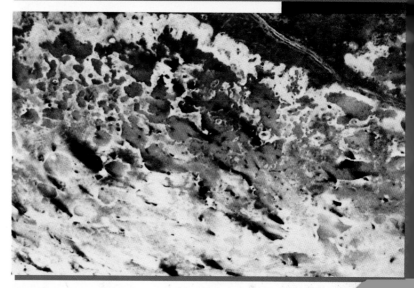

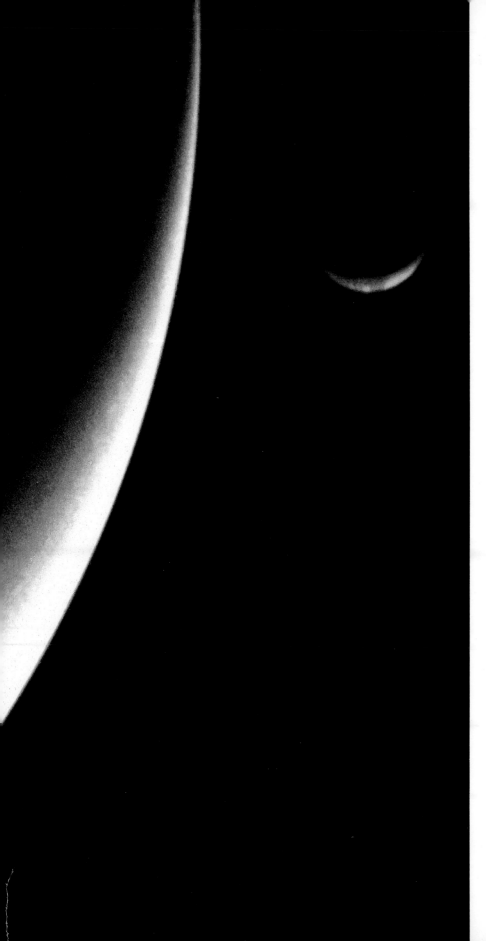

Parts of Triton are covered by pale ice caps. At first, scientists couldn't explain the dark streaks they saw on the ice. But as they looked at more pictures, they saw that dark jets of ice and gas were shooting up from the surface and then were being carried sideways by the wind. These jets, called geysers, occur when liquid below the surface explodes up through weak spots in the ice—like a warm soft drink when you pop open the can. Some geysers may erupt for months, spraying ice and gas miles into Triton's thin atmosphere and leaving dark streaks on its icy surface.

Ice geysers had never been seen before. This discovery, on the coldest moon in the solar system, was an exciting end to a 12-year adventure. Three days after leaving Triton, *Voyager* was already 3 million miles away. As it sped away, it gave scientists this last look at Neptune and Triton. It was not long before the last giant planet was just a dot in the distance.

◄ *Voyager's* last look at Neptune and Triton.

The *Voyagers* are still traveling.

Since leaving Saturn, *Voyager* 1 has been heading north out of the solar system. *Voyager* 2 is now heading south. Although the *Voyagers* are no longer taking pictures, they are still collecting data. They will continue to radio information back to Earth until about the year 2020. Both spacecraft are studying the solar wind, high energy particles that stream out of the Sun. And they are searching for the edge of the solar system—the place where our Sun's influence ends.

The *Voyagers* won't stop there. They will continue on into interstellar space, the empty space between the stars. Although they are traveling at more than 35,000 miles per hour, neither spacecraft will come near another star for thousands and thousands of years.

It is very unlikely that either *Voyager* will be found by space travelers from another world. But just in case, they carry a message from their home planet, Earth. A copper record attached to the side of the spacecraft contains pictures and sounds from Earth. It begins:

> "This is a present from a small and distant world,
> a token of our sounds, our science, our images,
> our music, our thoughts, and our feelings."

The *Voyagers* are still traveling, heading toward the stars, carrying a message from all of us.

► The record attached to each *Voyager* contains greetings in more than 60 languages, music from many different cultures, and other sounds from Earth, such as the songs of humpback whales. The record's cover (*inset*) has symbols showing where Earth is located in the universe.